T0122252

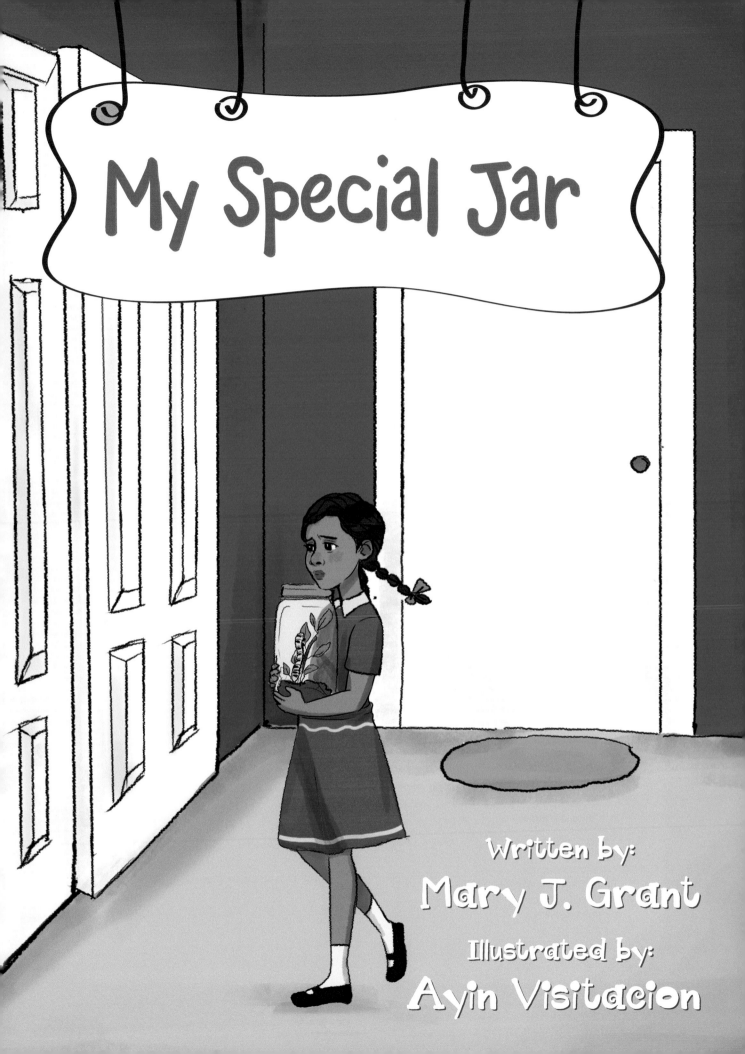

My Special Jar

Written by:
Mary J. Grant

Illustrated by:
Ayin Visitacion

ISBN: Softcover   978-1-7960-2657-3
          EBook   978-1-7960-2656-6

Print information available on the last page

Rev. date: 04/16/2019

To order additional copies of this book, contact:
Xlibris
1-888-795-4274
www.Xlibris.com
Orders@Xlibris.com
marygrant1915@gmail.com

My Special Jar

Ring! Ring! Ring! The dismissal bell rang very loud. I rushed to meet my sister, Nancy near the Wogamen Elementary School Library. I waited and waited and she never showed up, I was very sad.

I took a shortcut home. I was all alone and very frightened. I started running through wild bushes and tall grasses.

I jumped over a spiked barbed wire fence.

I landed on the path near some beautiful yellow wildflowers.

I picked one up and there was a caterpillar on a green leafy stick.

I thought to myself. I am going to take this special stick home.

I walked into the house with my special stick. I took some dirt, the caterpillar on the green leafy stick and placed it in a tall jar with holes in the top.

I took my special jar and put it in the living room.

Mother asked, "Who put this dirty jar in the living room?"

"Me!" I said.

I took my special jar and placed it on the kitchen counter.

Nancy asked, "Who put this nasty jar on the kitchen counter?"

"Me!" I said.

I took my special jar and placed it under the kitchen table.

Sis asked, "Who put this icky jar under the kitchen table?"

"Me!" I said.

I took my special jar and placed it in the bathroom.

Daddy asked, "Who put this grimy jar in the bathroom?"

"Me!" I said.

I took my special jar to the hallway closet.

Tootsie, asked, "Who put this weird jar in the hallway closet?"

"Me!" I said.

I sat on the attic step with my special jar. The caterpillar looked different. It had a covering on it.

I took it upstairs to the attic where no one could see it.

Every day I visited my special jar. I wondered when it was going to change again.

One day, I noticed that the covering was cracked just a little. I opened the curtain wider for more sunlight.

On my last visit to the attic, something happened. "Oh No!" I shouted, "It has two wings, six legs, two eyes, and two antennae."

I ran to get Daddy. He followed me to the attic and as I opened the door, he said, "Take that jar outside!"

I took the jar outside. I opened the jar and out flew an insect.

I screamed, "Sunshine!"

Daddy said, "First it was a caterpillar, next it became a cocoon and now it is a butterfly."

The butterfly flew around and then came back. It landed on my finger for a few seconds. I watched as it flew far away.

I went back into the house and everyone wanted to know what had happened. I shared my experience of my very special jar. Everyone looked at me with astonishment. They were so surprised to hear what had happened.

"Now, I can share my butterfly Sunshine with the world," I said.

"My Very Special Little Butterfly"
Song by Mary J. Grant
(Sung to the tune of "This Little Light of Mine")

First, it was a caterpillar,
Sliding all around,
First, it was a caterpillar,
Sliding all around,
First, it was a caterpillar,
Sliding around,
Sliding around,
Sliding around.

Then it became a cocoon,
Hanging off a stick,
Then it became a cocoon,
Hanging off a stick,
Then it became a cocoon.
Hanging off a stick,
On a stick,
On a stick,
On a stick.

This little butterfly of mine,
I'm going to let it fly,
This little butterfly of mine,
I'm going to let it fly,
This little butterfly of mine,
I'm going to let it fly,
Let it fly,
Let it fly,
Let it fly.

LIFE CYCLE OF "SUNSHINE" THE CATERPILLAR

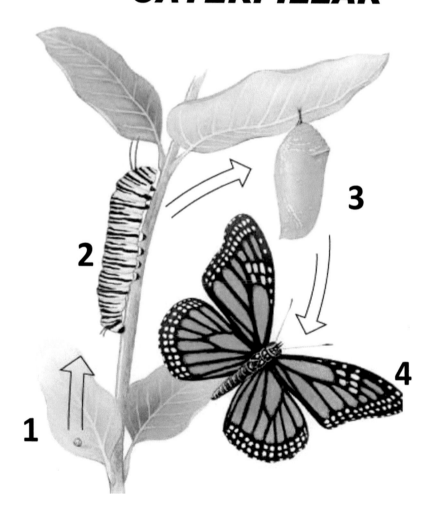

1. Egg
2. Caterpillar
3. Pupa
4. Butterfly

ABOUT THE AUTHOR

 Mary J. Grant is an author, educator and storyteller who has devoted her career to educating children.

As a teacher, supervisor and administrator, she always reminded her students that knowledge is power. Reading, writing and learning have always been her passion and a significant part of her life.

She is the author of three books, "My Daddy Taught Me To Read", "Floyd B's Pond" and "Shadows on Sunday." Each book has Maymay as the main character and members of her family are supporting characters.

She is a professional storyteller and has told engaging stories to adults and children all over the United States.

Please visit her website - www.storiesbymary.com

marygrant1915@gmail.com

Printed in the United States
By Bookmasters